I'm a one-eyed pirate.
Take a look!

In this costume
I'm Captain Hook.

I'm a fairy princess —
can't you tell?

I'll wave my wand
and cast a magic spell!

Ghosts and witches
don't scare me.

I'm a firefighter —
brave as can be.

Pumpkins, pumpkins everywhere!

My baby sister has one to wear!

What am I?
Can't you see?

I'm a colorful clown —
silly me!

I'm all set for
trick-or-treat—
lots of candies
and goodies to eat!

Happy **H**alloween!

Everett Anderson's Goodbye

PRESENTED TO

Howard Community College

by

HoCoPoLitSo

Everett Anderson's Goodbye

by Lucille Clifton
illustrated by
Ann Grifalconi

Holt, Rinehart and Winston | New York

Text copyright © 1983 by Lucille Clifton
Illustrations copyright © 1983 by Ann Grifalconi
All rights reserved, including the right to reproduce
this book or portions thereof in any form.
Published by Holt, Rinehart and Winston,
383 Madison Avenue, New York, New York 10017.
Published simultaneously in Canada by Holt, Rinehart
and Winston of Canada, Limited.

Library of Congress Cataloging in Publication Data
Clifton, Lucille, 1936–
   Everett Anderson's goodbye.
   Summary: Everett Anderson has a difficult time
coming to terms with his grief after his father dies.
   [1. Stories in rhyme. 2. Death—Fiction. 3. Fathers
and sons—Fiction] I. Grifalconi, Ann, ill. II. Title.
PZ8.3.C573Evh 1983   [E]   82-23426
ISBN 0-03-063518-7

Printed in the United States of America
10 9 8 7 6 5 4 3

ISBN 0-03-063518-7

for my sad friends

1 Denial
2 Anger
3 Bargaining
4 Depression
5 Acceptance

The Five Stages of Grief

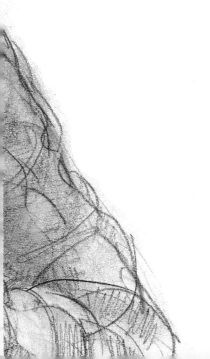

1

Everett Anderson holds the hand
of his mama until he falls asleep
and dreams about Daddy
in his chair, and
at the park, and
everywhere.
Daddy always laughing or never,
just Daddy, Daddy, forever and ever.

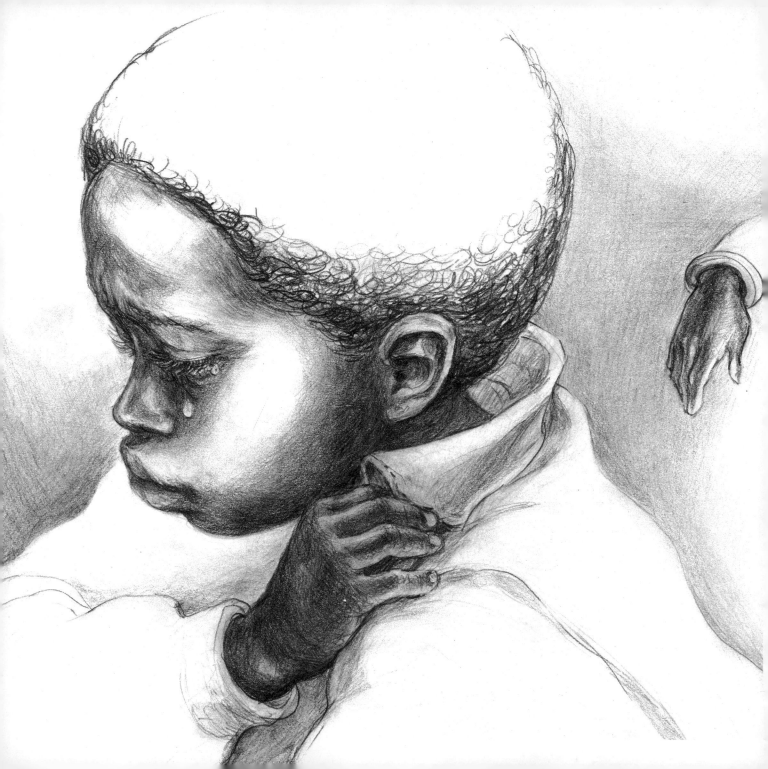

2

"I don't love Baby Evelyn
and I don't love Mr. Perry, too,
and I don't love Christmas or
Santa Claus
and I don't love candy
and I don't love you!"

"Well, Everett," his mama sighs,
"who do you love?"

And he cries and cries.

3

"I promise to learn my
  nine times nine
  and never sleep late or
  gobble my bread
  if I can see Daddy
  walking, and talking, and
  waving his hand, and
  turning his head.

"I will do everything you say
  if Daddy can be alive today."

4

Everett Anderson tries to sleep
but it is too hard and
the hurt is too deep.

Everett Anderson likes his food
but how can a dinner
do any good?

Everett Anderson just sits staring,
wondering what's the use of caring.

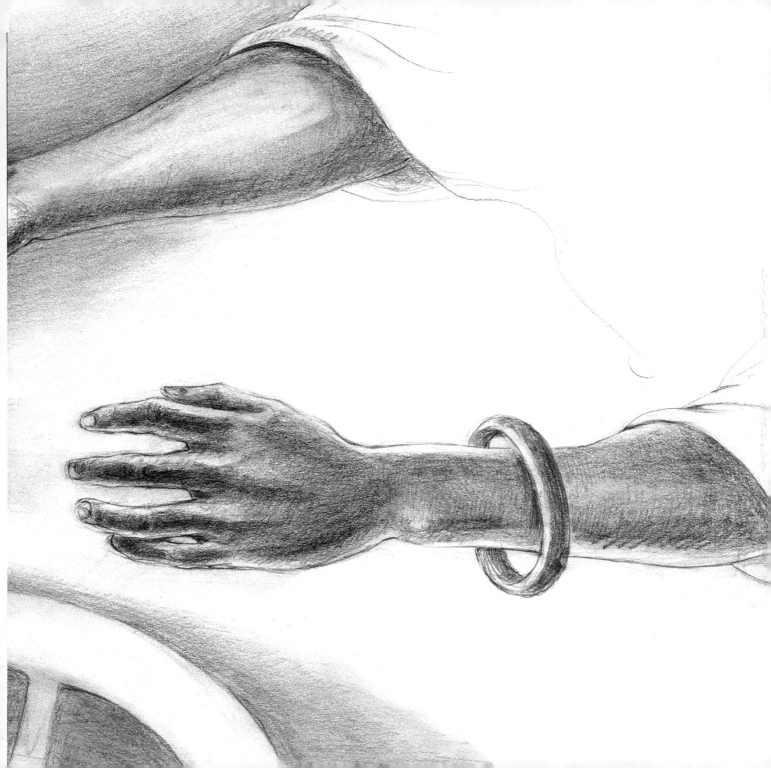

5

After a little bit of time

Everett Anderson says, "I knew
my daddy loved me through and through,
and whatever happens when people die,

love doesn't stop, and
neither will I."